A Trailblazer Curriculum Guide

JULIA PFERDEHIRT
WITH DAVE & NETA JACKSON

BETHANY HOUSE PUBLISHERS
MINNEAPOLIS, MINNESOTA 55438

CONTENTS

Copyright © 2000
Julia Pferdehirt with Dave and Neta Jackson

Illustrations © 2000
Bethany House Publishers

Published by Bethany House Publishers
A Ministry of Bethany Fellowship International
11400 Hampshire Ave. South
Minneapolis, Minnesota 55438
www.bethanyhouse.com
ISBN 0-7642-2345-3
Printed in the United States of America by
Bethany Press International, Minneapolis, Minnesota 55438

HOW TO USE THIS GUIDE

Welcome to the TRAILBLAZER BOOKS Curriculum Guides! As a teacher or homeschooling parent, you're glad when you see your students with their noses in books. But a good story is only the beginning of a learning adventure. Since the TRAILBLAZER BOOKS take readers all over the world into different cultures and time periods, each book opens a door to an exciting, humanities-based study that includes geography, history, social studies, literature, and language arts.

This Curriculum Guide for *The Hidden Jewel* about Amy Carmichael puts a host of activities and resources at your fingertips to help launch your students on a journey of discovery. The wealth of options allows you to choose the best pace and content for your students. You might want to assign students to simply read the book and then do one or two projects on folklore or food, travel or topography. Or you can delve deeper, planning a two-week unit with daily reading and vocabulary, research, creative writing, and hands-on projects. *Advance planning is key to effective use of this guide.*

SCOPE AND SEQUENCE

This guide includes **seven lessons**, enough for a two-week unit. The first and last lessons cover one chapter and provide historical background; all other lessons cover two chapters. All lessons include vocabulary, background information, discussion questions, and suggested activities. **Activities** are grouped by subject matter in the back of this guide: Geography (GEO), History (HIS), Social Studies and Folkways (SS/FW), and Literature and Language Arts (LIT/LA). Within each subject, look for symbols indicating different types of activities (writing, research, speech, reading, hands-on projects, video). Activities and resources particularly appropriate for younger or older students are designated as follows: younger (*), older (**). A three- to five-day Mega Project is also included. All activities list resources and materials needed.

PLANNING

Four to six weeks prior to the study . . .
- Skim *The Hidden Jewel*, review lessons

(pages 4–10), and choose activities, noting materials needed.

- Reserve materials on interlibrary loan and order films from specialty sources. (Titles and authors are listed in the **Activities** sections; full publication information is available under **Resources** on page 23 of this guide.)
- Purchase craft materials.

If you are planning a two-week unit . . .

- Students will cover one lesson daily for seven days.
- Choose one or more short, focused activities to accompany each lesson. Activities especially appropriate to the chapter(s) covered are noted on each lesson page.
- The remaining days can be devoted to the **Mega Projects** found on pages 17 and 22.

Note: Choose activities based on the age level, interests, and learning needs of your student(s). You might choose one activity from each discipline during the unit, *or* you might opt to balance the different types of activities.

LESSONS

- Assign relevant chapters in *The Hidden Jewel* the day before the lesson, to be read either individually *or* out loud as a family.
- **Praise and Prayer**, written by TRAILBLAZER authors Dave and Neta Jackson, provides an opportunity for students to spend a short time in God's Word and apply Scriptural concepts to their own lives.
- Read aloud the **Background** segment, then discuss **Vocabulary and Concepts**. (*Or* ask students to use context clues and a dictionary to define unfamiliar words as they read, leaving puzzling words or concepts to discuss the following day.)
- Give students an opportunity to discuss thoughts and reactions to their reading using the questions in the **Talk About It** feature. Discussion, debate, and interaction can be lively. Enjoy!
- Use the suggested **Activities**, or one of your own choosing.

Note: Unless marked otherwise, page and chapter numbers refer to Dave and Neta Jackson's original TRAILBLAZER BOOK *The Hidden Jewel*.

HISTORICAL SUMMARY

India is like a colorful garden. The world's highest mountains form one border, and a desert so bleak it is called "moonland" forms another. Hindu, Buddhist, Jain, and Muslim religious festivals are celebrated. Music, dance, and art reflect the culture's roots in China, Africa, and the Middle East. Even world-traveler Mark Twain said he dreamed of India and longed to return.

India was once an ancient, advanced culture. Indian astronomers and mathematicians were years ahead of their peers in Europe. Vaccination, algebra, geometry, and chess all came from India.

Then in the 1500s, British traders arrived. The British government began the East India Company to sell British goods in India and buy Indian goods for England.

British companies built factories in India. Prices were high and wages low. When the people protested, British soldiers confiscated their land. Finally, the Indian government was pushed aside, and England took over. Free India became a British colony.

In Amy Carmichael's time, Indian farmers paid half their earnings in taxes. Those who couldn't pay had to sell their land.

England taxed firewood, salt, and even schools! The poor were forced to heat and cook with cow dung. Schools that couldn't pay taxes closed, leaving Indian children without education. In time, India was no longer a cultural leader.

Amy Carmichael's India was owned and ruled by England. British people lived in separate, luxurious neighborhoods where only British schools and shops were built. British ways were "good" and Indian ways "bad."

British law was the ultimate authority. Indian customs and local laws were permitted as long as England's control was not threatened and British traders and businessmen still became wealthy. Indian practices like selling children to temples or marriages were ignored.

One bright spot in this picture of British power and Indian poverty is that missionaries were welcome. Many Christians longed to bring the Gospel to India. Some missionaries lived in the separate British compounds and only ventured out to preach to Indians. Others, like Amy Carmichael, lived among and like the Indian people.

Lesson One

CHAPTER 1: INCIDENT ON THE COG TRAIN

PRAISE AND PRAYER: GOD ACCEPTS EVERYONE

For hundreds of years, Indian society was organized by the *caste system* promoted by the Hindu religion, which said that some people were better than others. How does this compare with the teachings of the Bible? **Read Acts 10:34–35; James 2:1–9; and Revelation 22:17.** There is a saying that the ground is level at the foot of the cross. What do you think this means? Why does Christianity say all people are equal before God?

Thought: If we cannot depend on our own goodness to find favor with God, then we must depend on His gift of grace through Jesus' death (Ephesians 2:8–9).

Prayer: Help me, God, to show no favoritism in how I relate to others.

VOCABULARY AND CONCEPTS

magistrate, civil duties, gaunt, cog train

BACKGROUND

According to *Enchantment of the World: India* by Sylvia McNair, the Hindu religion divides people into groups, or castes. Each caste has a role and place in society. Each person is responsible to live morally and accept his or her place. Good deeds are rewarded by being reincarnated (reborn) into a higher and better caste. Punishment for sin is to be reincarnated as a lower caste.

The top caste was *Brahmans* (priests or scholars), then *Kshatriyas* (rulers and warriors), *Vaisyas* (tradespeople and farmers), and *Sudras* (servants and ordinary workers). The lowest-caste people swept streets, transported dead bodies, or tanned animal hides. They were called *untouchables* and were not allowed even to touch people of upper castes. They were supposed to accept this as punishment for sin in a past life. They hoped for a better life "next time."

Although the caste system has been outlawed for more than fifty years, old attitudes die hard. Today, most wealthy, well-educated people come from Brahman caste families. Although only a tiny percentage of the population is Brahman, more than half of all government officials come from this caste. In rural areas some people are still treated as untouchable.

"Stop!" John yelled. "A man just fell from the top of the train!"

TALK ABOUT IT

On page 15, John's father says, *"My job as an official of the British government is to rule and bring order to the country, while letting the natives take care of their own social affairs."* Do you think government can rule and still stay out of people's "social affairs"? How does government interfere with or control people's lives and relationships? Why do you think this is necessary or unnecessary?

ACTIVITIES

GEO 1; HIS 1

Lesson Two

CHAPTER 2: REPRIEVE FROM SCHOOL
CHAPTER 3: THE MONEY-BEGGING ELEPHANT

PRAISE AND PRAYER: AVOIDING OFFENSE

There are things we do or don't do because of our convictions about what pleases God. There are other things we do or don't do so as not to offend someone else. **Read Romans 14:13–23.** Name three things you do out of respect for other people even though God does not require them (possibly manners).

Thought: Not offending other people about customs sometimes gives us the opportunity to tell them about Jesus (1 Corinthians 9:22–23).

Prayer: God, though some people may reject me because I follow you, please help me not to offend them unnecessarily.

VOCABULARY AND CONCEPTS

reprieve, unyielding, salaam, paganism, moderate, thatch-roof huts, compound, Tamil

BACKGROUND

British officials, merchants, and army officers sometimes settled their families in India. Some children literally grew up in India. Others were sent back to England to attend boarding schools. Schools like Kingsway School for Boys, mentioned in chapter 2, were scattered throughout India. The sons of wealthy British families could attend "proper" British schools. The buildings were even constructed to *look* like traditional British boarding schools. In spite of the heat, students were required to wear jackets and ties like boys back in chilly England. The surrounding Indian culture was considered peculiar at best and its people inferior.

The caste system influenced every part of Indian life. In chapter 3, note that Hindus and Muslims did not even drink water from the same jar. Servants could do only jobs allowed for their caste. On trains, each caste rode in a different section. Amy Carmichael always rode third class, declaring that since Jesus made no caste distinctions, neither would she.

John decided not to ask his mother whether giving money to a pagan temple [elephant] was a good thing.

TALK ABOUT IT

John felt uncomfortable giving coins to the temple elephant. Why? Have you ever been in a situation where you did something commonly accepted or even expected, only to feel uncomfortable about it later? (*Note*: Let students wrestle with their own ideas. Suggest this example if necessary: A child might visit a friend's home where grace isn't said before meals. Does she pray and possibly embarrass the family or do as they do?)

ACTIVITIES

GEO 2, 3, 4; LIT/LA 10

Lesson Three

CHAPTER 4: REFUGE!
CHAPTER 5: GOOD FRIDAY COMES ON EASTER

PRAISE AND PRAYER: GOD'S BRIDE FOR ISAAC

Arranged marriages seem odd to our Western culture. We expect to make our own choices. But they were common in Bible times. **Read Genesis 24.** Abraham's servant went to find a bride for Isaac, but according to verses 7, 12, 27, 40, and 44, who did the real arranging? Still, choice mattered. See verses 8, 57, and 58.

Thought: A wise Christian seeks God's guidance in finding the spouse he has prepared for him or her.

Prayer: Dear Lord, prepare for me a spouse who will help me serve you, and help me recognize who that person is when the time comes.

VOCABULARY/CONCEPTS

refuge, urgent, sari, dung

On page 53, what does Sanford Knight mean when he says, "interfering with the domestic affairs of the Indian people"?

> Arul bent down and lifted the girl to her feet. "Refuge! She wants refuge."

BACKGROUND

"Jewel" arrived at Dohnavur wearing beautiful gold jewelry on her hands, wrists, ankles, and ears. Her nose may have been pierced to display a beautiful gold ring. Jewelry meant a woman was the daughter, wife, or mother of a wealthy man. Ear piercing was (and is) common for both boys and girls. Long ago, when knowledge and teaching were passed from person to person orally, ear piercing was believed to sharpen children's hearing and increase their ability to learn.

Jewel's father, a wealthy merchant, probably made his money running factories to make goods for British trade. Cloth and machinery were important trade items. The British and Indian merchants became wealthy, but their wealth was obtained by paying Indian workers so little they were virtually slaves.

Chapter 5 tells of spreading cow dung on a floor. Dung was used for more than "plaster." Because British manufacturers made beautiful furniture from Indian wood, the government wanted to keep Indian people from cutting trees. They taxed firewood, forcing people to use dried cow dung for cooking fuel instead. Small grill-like braziers burned dung for heat.

TALK ABOUT IT

How did reading about Jewel and her uncle make you feel? Why do you think Indian tradition allows for arranged marriages? What do you think of the idea that someone could be forced to marry whether they wanted to or not?

ACTIVITIES

SS/FW 2, 3, 4, 5

Lesson Four

CHAPTER 6: SWAMI-LOVER

CHAPTER 7: FIRE!

PRAISE AND PRAYER: BECOMING ONE IN CHRIST

It seems we humans tend to divide ourselves from people who are different. **Read Galatians 3:26–28 and Ephesians 2:11–22.** According to these passages, are you closer to a Christian of another race on the other side of the world, or an unbelieving neighbor who looks nearly the same as you do? Explain your answer.

Thought: According to John 17:20–21, Jesus deeply desires that all believers become one, no matter what our race, nationality, or cultural backgrounds.

Prayer: O Lord, help me remember how you prayed for me in John 17 and not go against your will for me by separating myself from other Christians.

VOCABULARY AND CONCEPTS

monsoon
What does "My father is commissioned as magistrate" on page 62 mean?
What does "petitioning the court" on page 68 mean?

BACKGROUND

In Amy Carmichael's time, Indian buildings were sometimes brick. Most village houses were built from a cement-like mix of straw, clay, and cow dung packed between forms to harden into walls. The walls were whitewashed if a family had enough money. Thatch roofs like those described in *The Hidden Jewel* were common.

This house-building technique was a clever use of cheap, easily obtained materials. Termites would eat wood, and brick was expensive. The clay-straw-dung mixture built a house that was cool in the hot season and retained heat on cold nights. Thatch roofs were built from straw and dried grasses. They kept the rain out and were porous enough to allow moisture to evaporate.

Azim
looked
startled
when John
spoke
Tamil.

TALK ABOUT IT

When the judge gave Jewel into Miss Carmichael's care until the final court decision was made, Jewel's uncle insisted the girl must "keep caste." Why? What would be the result if Jewel did not obey? (Note: If Jewel failed to keep caste by associating with lower-caste people, she would be shamed and considered unworthy for marriage. The uncle would lose his moneymaking opportunity.)

In America people were once criticized and shunned for marrying outside their race. Interracial marriages were illegal in some states. How is the American history of racism like the caste system? How is it different?

ACTIVITIES

LIT/LA 2, 3, 4; HIS 2, 3; SS/FW 6, 7

Lesson Five

Chapter 8: A Bloody Nose and a Black Eye
Chapter 9: On Trial

PRAISE AND PRAYER: HUMBLE YOURSELF

It is common to slip into rude and disrespectful behavior. Maybe that is because we have felt the hurt of someone insulting us and we think it will make us feel better if we pass it on. **Read 1 Peter 2:13–17; 3:8–12; and 5:5–7.** How have you felt when you returned "evil for evil" or passed it on to someone else?

Thought: According to Hebrews 11:25, sin sometimes brings satisfaction for a short period of time. But why doesn't it last?

Prayer: Help me not to exchange the short-term pleasure of insulting other people for the long-term regret of having made enemies of them.

VOCABULARY AND CONCEPTS

tunic, rupees, telegram
On page 97, what does "the judgment" mean?

BACKGROUND

The history in these chapters is not pretty. In the fictional story of John's fight with Jim, we read that the headmaster did nothing to punish the boys for turning their backs and walking out on John's friend Mr. Rabur.

One of the reasons for this attitude—which would not have been held by everyone, of course—was that British people considered the Indians inferior. In 1900, India had been "sucked dry" after more than two hundred years of British rule. Taxes were high. British companies owned most factories and natural resources. Most Indians were not cultured and clean like the British; they were poor and illiterate. Some British people decided being poor and illiterate meant people must also be lazy and worthless. The result of this sad situation was racism.

Unfortunately, racism was part of Indian culture, too. The caste system actually had rules to be sure that lower-caste people did not mix with upper-caste people. Even today, light-skinned Indians are often considered more attractive.

"John! What happened to your eye? And whatever are you wearing?"

TALK ABOUT IT

Chapter 8 reveals the cruelty and disrespect of John's classmates toward Mr. Rabur. Hold a family, class, or homeschool group discussion about racism.

Here are some starter questions: Why did John's classmates walk out on Mr. Rabur? Was that the first time the boys had shown disrespect to Mr. Rabur? Give some examples. Have you ever seen someone be treated with disrespect because of his or her color? Gender? Age? Talk about what you observed and thought.

ACTIVITIES

LIT/LA 4, 5, 11, 12

Lesson Six

CHAPTER 10: **DISAPPEARED!**

CHAPTER 11: **DISCOVERED**

PRAISE AND PRAYER: OBEYING GOD

The Bible instructs us to obey the rulers over us. **Read Romans 13:1–5 and 1 Peter 2:13–17.** Yet throughout the history of the Church (from the stoning of Stephen in Acts 7 to the modern martyrs), Christians have been killed for disobeying the authorities over them. How can this be? **Read Acts 5:27–32.** What gave Peter and the other apostles the right to disobey their rulers?

Thought: It is never right to disobey a human law unless we are doing so in order to obey God's laws. Then we *must* obey God rather than humans.

Prayer: O Lord, help me to have the courage to obey you when others laugh at me or even if they threaten me and make laws saying I can't obey you.

VOCABULARY AND CONCEPTS

bandy, ferry, cable (telegram), plight

On page 110, what does "a hasty disguise" mean?

BACKGROUND

When a person decides to break a law that seems wrong or unjust, it is called civil disobedience. That is what John and Miss Beath plan in these chapters.

In America, many people chose civil disobedience during the 1950s and 1960s. When the law said black people were not allowed to eat in restaurants, black and white students entered restaurants and politely asked to be served. They refused to leave, even though they knew police would come and arrest them.

In India, Mohandas Gandhi also did many acts of civil disobedience. He was determined to use peaceful means to free India from English rule. Once, the British government put a high tax on salt. People were not even allowed to gather salt near the ocean! Mohandas Gandhi and other Indians walked hundreds of miles to the ocean and each picked up a handful of salt knowing they would go to jail.

> "John! John Knight! I can't believe it!" Amy Carmichael said.

TALK ABOUT IT

Civil disobedience is a subject Christians often disagree about. One person thinks pro-life groups are right to cut the electric lines to abortion clinics. Another thinks this is wrong. One Christian would go to prison rather than serve in the military. Another believes he or she must obey the government even if it means killing in war. Is one person right and the other wrong?

Talk about John's choice to break the law in *The Hidden Jewel.* Should he have broken the law to help Jewel? What other choices could John have made?

ACTIVITIES

GEO 5; LIT/LA 6, 7, 13, 14

Lesson Seven

CHAPTER 12: THE BRIDE OF DOHNAVUR MORE ABOUT AMY CARMICHAEL

PRAISE AND PRAYER: BASIC CHRISTLIKE LIVING

Sometimes it is good to review what are the minimum expectations God has for us, not that we should do only the minimum. But knowing what they are helps us put everything else in perspective. **Read Micah 6:8; James 1:22; and Matthew 22:37–40; 25:31–46.** Make a list of God's minimum expectations for us.

Thought: Though we are saved only by faith, God expects us to live like *his* children, like Jesus. Therefore, "What would Jesus do?" makes a good motto.

Prayer: Dear Lord, help me to keep the basics in mind so that I don't get distracted by other things—good though they might be.

VOCABULARY AND CONCEPTS

astounded
What does "so calloused" on page 121 mean?

The next moment the young woman and man turned toward John, and a flash of recognition surged through his body.

BACKGROUND

While India has changed since 1900, it still faces terrible problems. The caste system is forbidden by law, but most people still marry within their caste. People from the *pariah* or untouchable caste are still more likely to be homeless, uneducated, and poor. Hindus often receive better jobs and educational opportunities than their Sikh, Muslim, or Christian neighbors. Christians are often persecuted.

The practice of selling children to Hindu temples is outlawed today. But Indian women are second-class people. Poor families consider daughters a burden. Daughters earn little or no money. Marriage dowries are high. A poor family may spend precious rupees to send a son to the doctor or to school, but not a daughter. Abortion and even killing of infant girls is not uncommon. Like Amy Carmichael, Mother Teresa's Sisters of Charity care for unwanted girls.

TALK ABOUT IT

One woman once explained arranged marriages by saying, "We put a cold pot on a warm fire and it grows warm slowly. Americans put a hot pot on a cold fire and it slowly becomes cold."

Imagine, Arul and Jewel had not seen or spoken to each other in six years, and yet they agreed to an arranged marriage! Arranged marriages are common even today in India. Talk about this. List advantages and disadvantages of arranged marriages. Ask each person's opinion. Why do you think arranged marriages still occur in India? Why do you think they seldom occur in America?

ACTIVITIES

SS/FW 8, 9, 10, 11; CT 1

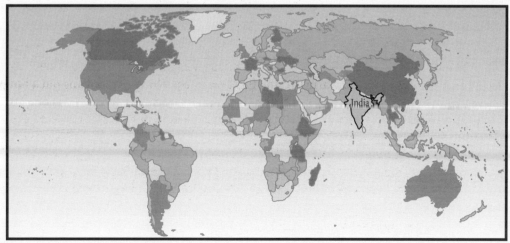

This page may be reproduced for in-home or in-class use.

Geography

If we know the land, we will know more about the people. In a land like India, bordered by ocean and mountains and containing jungle and desert, the land determines much about how people live.

As advances in technology (television, Internet, etc.) make our world smaller and smaller, students must know about other countries. To understand the news and politics, students must understand how and where people live around the world. So geography is more than finding India on a map; it involves understanding how the land affects people and culture.

 GEO 1: Look through books and magazines for photos of India. How many different land environments can you find? Check books and the Internet for pictures of the Great Indian Desert and the Himalayan Mountains. (RESEARCH)

 GEO 2: Using clay or papier-mâché, construct a raised relief map of India. Clays of different color or paint on papier-mâché will help show mountains, desert areas, forest and jungle-like areas, and water. Put cities and railroad lines on the map. What do you notice about where people live and locate their transportation systems? (HANDS-ON)

 GEO 3: Geologists think India was once part of Africa. Under the crust of the earth are what geologists call tectonic plates. At Creation all land on earth may have begun in one place. (See Genesis 1:9.) Then the plates shifted, volcanoes erupted, oceans formed and changed. Just as God used volcanoes to form the Hawaiian Islands, he used the shifting of underground "plates" to shape the land. An example of land changing in this way is the San Andreas Fault on the Pacific coast, where a moving plate is pulling a piece of California into the ocean.

Find a map of tectonic plates in a book or encyclopedia or online. Notice where the plates lie. Notice the borders of Africa and South America. Notice the outlines of eastern Africa and India.

Copy a world map by hand or on a copy machine. Draw the tectonic plates on this map. Cut out the continents and see if you can fit them together like a puzzle. What does this tell you about creation? (HANDS-ON)

 GEO 4: Copy the map on page 11 of this guide. As you read, find the cities, rivers, and sites mentioned in *The Hidden Jewel* and record them on this map. (HANDS-ON)

 GEO 5: Trace John's journey from school in Ooty (now known as Udagamandalam) to Palamcottah (Palayankottai). Trace John and Jewel's journey to Colombo, Ceylon (Sri Lanka). Imagine traveling by third-class train through the Indian countryside, biking frantically to Four Lakes, and plodding in an oxcart toward Ceylon! (HANDS-ON)

 GEO 6: View *The Great Indian Railway* by National Geographic. One of a series showing especially beautiful or interesting railway trips around the world, this video shows the geography of India as well as its people. (VIDEO)

 GEO 7: Trace a map of India and all its neighboring countries. Label the many countries that border India or the nearby Indian Ocean. (HANDS-ON)

 GEO 8: Search old issues of *National Geographic* magazine and other travel and culture magazines, books, and the Internet for photos of Indian people, traditional clothing, and folkways. Cut photos when possible or make color photocopies. Internet photos can be downloaded and printed right on some home printers. Create a

geographical and cultural map by tracing India's outline on poster board. Use photos and drawings to show as many cultural/ethnic groups as you can. Glue cutouts and sketches around and on the map, showing where different ethnic groups live. (HANDS-ON)

 GEO 9: The Himalayan Mountains are one of India's great treasures. Check your library or search the Internet for information about the Himalayan Mountains. Find the Himalayan Mountains on a map. (RESEARCH)

 GEO 10: Michael Pollard's book *The Ganges* follows the Ganges River from the Himalayan Mountains to the Bay of Bengal. At each stop, the writer tells more of the history and culture of India. The Ganges is considered a holy river by Hindus. Farmers depend on water from the flooded Ganges during monsoon season for crops. Read *The Ganges* and write a summary of what you learn in each chapter. (WRITING)

 GEO 11: Read *The First Rains* by Peter Bonnici to learn about the monsoons. Tell what you learn to your family, class, or homeschool group. (READING)

 GEO 12: Check out any of the following *National Geographic* magazine articles:
- "A Himalayan Park" (June 1998)
- "Himalayan Caravans" (December 1993)
- "On the Rails in India" (May 1995)

Choose one article. Summarize what you learn and share it with your family, class, or homeschool group. (RESEARCH)

History

An old saying claims that people who don't know history are doomed to repeat it. Whether that is true or not, knowing history helps us to understand why people behave as they do, how governments work, and how one event causes another as history unfolds.

HIS 1: Using library books and online or print encyclopedias, learn about the caste system. Find out how the system worked in Indian communities. Write a report about what you learn. (RESEARCH)

HIS 2: Read *Gold Cord: The Story of a Fellowship* by Amy Carmichael to find out about the real Arul. Check the index for several stories about this boy who grew up and reached out to other orphaned and homeless boys at Dohnavur. (READING)

HIS 3: Read *The First Rains* by Peter Bonnici to learn about the monsoons. Tell what you learn to your family, class, or homeschool group. (*Note:* This activity is included here as well as in GEO 11 because the book not only talks about monsoons—a topic for geography—but also an important historical event.) (READING)

HIS 4: Enjoy the *National Geographic* magazine article "India: 50 Years of Independence" (May 1997). Read and take notes. Create an outline from your notes, article subheadings, and photograph captions to present an oral report on this article. (RESEARCH)

HIS 5:** (a project for older students) Read *India: A Study of an Economically Developing Country* by David Cumming to learn how India's history has affected its economy. How did the years as a colony affect India's economy today? Read "Indicators of Poverty" on page 19 of Cumming's book. How does knowing the number of doctors or the percentage of people who can read in India tell us about the poverty or wealth of the country? (READING)

HIS 6: In 1993 a terrible earthquake hit India. Repairs, like rebuilding schools and roads and digging new wells and sewers, cost about $90 million! This poor country had no "savings account" to rebuild their cities. The government borrowed money from wealthier countries like the United States. That money must be paid back.

In many poor countries, money needed to feed hungry people, educate children, or provide job training goes instead to pay old debts. Interest on loans is so high the debt can never be paid.

The Christian movement Jubilee 2000 is encouraging wealthy countries to cancel much of this debt. Learn about Jubilee online at www.j2000usa.org. (INTERNET)

HIS 7: View *Jubilee 2000 USA*, a twenty-four-minute video about debt in poor countries, available through Jubilee 2000 at www.j2000usa.org. (VIDEO)

HIS 8: People in India sometimes work long days at hard jobs and still cannot earn enough money to feed their families. Learn about world hunger at www.hungersite.com. Each time you visit this site, sponsoring organizations donate food to hungry people! (INTERNET)

HIS 9: Mohandas Gandhi helped free India. Study about him using library books, encyclopedias, and the Internet. Find out how Gandhi worked for peace as well as freedom. Read about his walk to protest the salt tax in India. (RESEARCH)

HIS 10: Mohandas Gandhi fought injustice with peace. When others were violent toward him, he refused to be violent in return. Read a biography about Gandhi and write a summary of what you learn. (READING)

 HIS 11: View the video *Something Beautiful for God.* (VIDEO)

Social Studies and Folkways

Folkways are the traditions of a people and culture. Art, foods, storytelling, music, dance, drama, literature, and even religion are mirrors reflecting the heart and soul of a nation and its people.

For Western people, understanding Asian culture, values, and traditions is especially challenging. Our cultures are very, very different. Yet, as Amy Carmichael discovered when she willingly gave up British ways to adopt Indian clothing, traditions, and lifestyle, when we share the traditions of our neighbors, they become friends.

SS/FW 1: On page 23, girls from Dohnavur Fellowship greet John by placing their palms together and bowing their heads. This is called a *salaam*. Talk about how this greeting shows respect. How do we greet people in America? Using books and asking questions, find out about traditions of greeting in other cultures.

(*Note:* Japanese people bow from the waist. Some Muslim people place a hand over the heart. Some Native Americans lifted one hand, palm out.) (RESEARCH)

SS/FW 2: Read *Teenage Refugees and Immigrants From India Speak Out* by R. Viswanath. This book is written in the words of young people from India today. Some girls say they expect their marriage will be arranged by their parents. Other girls mention arranged marriage as a problem in their lives. (READING)

SS/FW 3: Put on a sari! Saris are dresses worn by many Indian women. Some are colorful and bright and the fabric can be beautiful.

You'll need a length of 36-inch-wide fabric about 4 to 4½ yards long, a short-sleeved knit shirt, and an ankle-length half-slip.

1. Put on slip and T-shirt.
2. Hold the cloth lengthwise. Tuck one end into the waistband of the slip, starting in front and working your way counter-clockwise until you reach your right hip.
3. Pull the end of the loose cloth over your left shoulder. It should drape down your back to your knees.
4. Pleat this loose piece, folding it back and forth like a fan until it forms a "skirt" about the size of your waist. Then you'll be able to neatly tuck the folded cloth into the waistband.
5. Your T-shirt will cover your arms, chest, and back. The cloth draped over your shoulder creates a pretty shawl-like look. The skirt may be pinned to keep it secure.

(HANDS-ON)

SS/FW 4: At Dohnavur children played games, did chores and schoolwork, and met for worship and Bible study. One game they might have played is Kabaddi. Here are the rules so you can play:

You'll need two teams. One player runs into the other team's territory. The player must chase the opposing players and touch as many as possible. Each "touch" is worth a point.

The trick is, the player must chase and tag opponents and make it back to his or her own base *in a single breath*!

No cheating! Indian Kabaddi players must prove they are not sneaking a second breath by repeating the word "kabaddi" over and over until they run out of breath or reach their own base! (*Kabaddi* is a nonsense word used for this game.) (HANDS-ON)

SS/FW 5: Check this Web site and links on the Internet to learn about Tamil culture and language: www.geocities.com/Athens/5180. (INTERNET)

SS/FW 6: Find a photo of a thatch-roofed Indian home in a book or magazine. Using clay or salt dough, make a model of that house. Use white tempera or other water-based paint as whitewash. Include as many details in this model as possible. For example, note how windows and doors are made. Does the family cook outside in a clay oven? Is the courtyard brick or dirt? Is the home surrounded by a fence or wall? Look closely at the thatch roof. Using pieces of straw or dried, brown grasses (such as those found in prairie restoration areas or in meadows), tie bundles of "thatch" together to recreate the roof. If you can find photos of people wearing traditional Indian clothing in a magazine, cut them out and mount them on cardboard. Now you have "residents" for your model home.

Display and explain your model to your family, class, or homeschool group. (HANDS-ON)

MEGA PROJECT IDEAS: 7 and 8

 SS/FW 7: The entire Dohnavur Fellowship celebrated Jewel and Arul's wedding with a feast. So can you. Decorate your dining room with streamers and flowers. String real blossoms or tissue paper flower garlands for everyone. Younger children can cut and color banana leaves from butcher paper, since Indian people often use these long, shiny leaves as plates.

Visit a library to find Indian cookbooks. Plan, shop for, and prepare an Indian meal. Watch out! When a cookbook describes Indian food as spicy, it means really spicy!

Or make a simple vegetable curry by steaming chopped cauliflower and potatoes. Mix 1 teaspoon curry powder, 1/2 teaspoon cumin seeds, 1/4 teaspoon chili powder, 1 teaspoon turmeric, 1 teaspoon salt, and 1/2 teaspoon black mustard seeds. Pour into saucepan with 2 heaping tablespoons of tomato puree and 2/3 cup water. Simmer, stirring occasionally. Add potatoes and cauliflower and heat through. Serve on white rice, sprinkled with chopped parsley or coriander.

How about Indian ice cream for dessert?

You'll need 1 can sweetened condensed milk; 1 small can evaporated milk; 1 cup whipping cream, unwhipped; 1/2 cup almonds; 1/2 cup fruit (mango, berries, kiwi, strawberries, peaches, or bananas).

Mix on high in a blender until frothy and well blended. Mixture will thicken as cream whips. Pour into shallow dish with a lid and freeze until solid. Cut into slices, top with fruit, and enjoy! (COOKING)

 SS/FW 8: Before your feast, find out about Indian dining habits. Use books, encyclopedias, and online resources to learn how Indian people serve and eat food. Read or tell what you find as part of your Indian feast.

When you thank God for this food, remember the Indian word *pongol,* which means *overflowing.* God's blessings to us are pongol. (RESEARCH)

 SS/FW 9: Visit an Indian restaurant in your community. With prior arrangements, you may be able to tour the kitchen during prep-time before the restaurant opens. Ask the cook to explain how spices are used in Indian foods. Does the cook prepare a special type of Indian cuisine? (For example, Hindus never cook or eat meat. Muslims love Tandoori chicken but never eat pork.)

Be sure to stay for lunch! Indian families sometimes like to order many dishes to share. (HANDS-ON)

 SS/FW 10: Religion affects almost every part of Indian life. What people eat is determined by their religion. Clothing, marriage arrangements, and politics are influenced by religion. Almost every holiday involves some religious observance.

Learn about what Hindus, Muslims, Sikhs, or Jains believe. Find out about their traditions and practices. Your library will have books, videos, encyclopedias, or Web sites to suggest.

Write a report about this religion to present to your family, class, or homeschool group. Include pictures when possible.

(*Note*: When exposing students to non-Christian religions, one challenge is to communicate respect for other people and cultures while affirming the truth that only Jesus offers salvation and the way to God. Words like *heathen* or *pagan* can be dismissive and fail to acknowledge that people following other religions often *want* to be right with God, yet cannot find him. Amy Carmichael understood people who honestly wanted to find God and be holy, but without Jesus were always trying and always failing to earn their way to God, perfection, and heaven. Understanding is more than knowing why Jesus is God and Buddha isn't. Understanding leads to compassion and a missionary's heart. Understanding reveals the great, undeserved gift of forgiveness in Christ in contrast to the fear and uncertainty resulting from works-based religious philosophies.) (WRITING)

 SS/FW 11: Indian artists are famous for their delicate brass and silver artwork. Visit an import shop where Indian brass platters, lamps, jewelry, or other artwork is sold. Ask the shopkeeper if you can gather samples of metal art by making rubbings of the articles using charcoal or black crayon and large sheets of butcher paper. Collect and display rubbings of as many kinds of metalwork as you can find. (HANDS-ON)

 SS/FW 12: Obtain a tape or CD of Indian music at your library or music store and listen to it while you work on activities from this guide. (MUSIC)

 SS/FW 13: Invite an Indian person to visit your class or homeschool group to share about life, traditions, culture, and/or politics in India today. Be sure to read about Indian life in books or on-line and prepare questions for your guest.

(*Note:* Area churches, universities, or Indian-owned businesses may be contact points for names of people willing to address a group of young people.) (RESEARCH)

SS/FW 14: Indians invented the game of chess! Read *The Token Gift* by Hugh McKibbon about this interesting game. Learn to play it yourself. (HANDS-ON)

Literature and Language Arts

Stories are windows to understanding people and their culture. When we enjoy folktales or listen to song lyrics from another culture, we see and appreciate the creativity of the people.

Reading books set in another culture, like *The Hidden Jewel,* also makes us better writers. We see how words are used to tell a story, describe a scene, or reveal a character. Students can experiment, using those techniques in their own writing.

LIT/LA 1: Use books and online sources to find out about the Tamil language. At www.tamil.org copies of Tamil script can be found. Copy some script and, using a felt marker and paper, try your hand at writing Tamil. You may also find examples of Hindi script to copy. The writing is very beautiful. (HANDS-ON)

LIT/LA 2: View *Carol's Mirror,* a video about a young black girl who wants the lead role in the school play, *Snow White.* This video is an interesting window into the experience of people of color in our world today. Rent from MCC Resource Library, Akron, PA. (717) 859-1151. (VIDEO)

LIT/LA 3: Read "Rikki Tikki Tavi" aloud as a family. This well-known tale about a mongoose, two cobras, and a British family in India was written for children back home in England. (This story is available in numerous editions.) (READING)

LIT/LA 4: Read one of the following books to help you slip inside the mind and feelings of a person living with racism. *Mister and Me* by Kimberly Willis Holt; *The Christmas Menorahs* by Janice Cohn; *Not Separate, Not Equal* by Brenda Wilkinson; *Sarah With an H* by Hadley Irwin; or *Prank* by Kathryn Lasky. (READING)

LIT/LA 5: Read aloud *The Sneetches,* a picture book by Dr. Suess. Talk about the symbol of the stars on the bellies of the Sneetches. How did Sneetches decide it was better to have stars than not have stars? Why did the "no star" Sneetches accept being kept off the beaches? Did getting stars make the situation any better?

Tell students that one reason Dr. Suess wrote *The Sneetches* was to help people see how racism begins and what it does to people. Ask students what they think of this. (READING)

LIT/LA 6:** In the 1960s a white man in America darkened his skin and traveled in the South as a black person. He wrote a book, *Black Like Me,* about his experiences. While this is an adult book and not appropriate for young readers, helpful insights about experiencing the world as a minority person might be gained if a teacher or parent pulled excerpts from this unusual book to share with students. (READING)

LIT/LA 7: On page 111 we read that John sent a postcard to Dohnavur, hoping to tell Amy Carmichael that he and Jewel were safe. He wrote a Bible verse on the card. Find that verse in Scripture. Read the whole chapter/section. Why do you think John chose that verse?

(*Note:* John was writing "in code." The idea of using the scripture as code has been used by Christians at different times in history. For example, Brother Andrew, the famous Bible smuggler, communicated with Christians who did not speak his language entirely through Bible verses! It will be interesting for students to share their theories about why John chose that particular verse.) (RESEARCH)

LIT/LA 8: Read *The Jungle Book* or *Just So Stories* by Rudyard Kipling. Either is a wonderful read-aloud. Also look for Robin McKinley's *Tales from*

the Jungle Book, a retelling of Kipling's stories. (READING)

LIT/LA 9: Find a traditional Indian folktale in your library in a collection of folklore or a book about Indian folktales. Either learn this folktale to tell to your family, class, or homeschool group or rewrite this folktale in your own words and illustrate your writing. Share what you have written with your family, class, or homeschool group.

(*Note:* Groups of students may be assigned to choose a folktale from a literary genre such as religious tales, animal tales, tales of magic, etc. Sharing folktales of different types in a group setting will open a broader window into Indian folklore.) (WRITING)

LIT/LA 10: On pages 17 and 18, we read about John's first visit to the British school in Ooty. Here is how this word picture is painted for us:

His father had been right—it looked very much like his old school back in Brighton, except, instead of the English Channel sparkling in the distance, the Western Ghats rose like a misty wall out of the foothills. Boys in blazers and school ties looked at him curiously and poked each other as the three Knights walked down the cool corridor. Once they had been ushered into the school office, however, it did not take them long to realize they had bumped into another type of wall: the headmaster.

Notice how the writers "paint" the scene by telling us about mountains "rising like a misty wall" and then introduce us to the headmaster by calling him a "wall." What do readers automatically think about the headmaster because of this one word? (Talk with students about their ideas.)

Assignment: Make a list of three objects. Then write one paragraph introducing a character that is like that object. Begin each paragraph by *showing* your character to readers. Use actions, words, and thoughts to show us what kind of person he or she is. Then in the final sentence, tell us your character's name and what

he or she is like.

(Example: He lit the lamp with trembling fingers and leaned back in his chair. He made a mental note to ask his son to carry the firewood in when he visited tomorrow. Years ago he could have split firewood all day. Now just a trip up and down the steps left him wheezing and shaking. A cup of tea would taste good, but he could not find the energy even to fill the kettle. Instead, he closed his eyes. Rest would be better than tea. What had happened? Years ago he was strong as an oak. Now John Clements was a dry, autumn leaf.) (WRITING)

LIT/LA 11: What an ending to chapter 9! Imagine yourself in John's situation: Your friend has just been sent to an uncle who will force her to marry an old man she does not love or even know—and your own father sent her! Worse, the law is on *their* side, not yours. What are you thinking? Feeling? What will you do?

You're going to enter this story as John, the main character. Writing in first person, tell what you think happens next (no reading ahead!). *Show* how John feels. Show what he is thinking. Does he make a list of options and compare them? Does he suddenly get a terrifying, almost impossible idea and decide to run with it— dangerous or not? Does he meet someone who helps?

Your goal in this writing is only to say what John does and what happens next. Don't resolve the whole story; our authors have already done that. Just "play" with the story by writing your own version of the next scene.

Remember, good writers tell the story from the point of view of the main character. They tell the story through their main character's feelings, thoughts, observations, and experiences. (WRITING)

LIT/LA 12: Another trick of good writing is called *show, don't tell.* Here's an example from chapter 9 of *The Hidden Jewel:*

Amy Carmichael…sat quietly on the other side of the room. Her hands were folded on the table in front of her, her face tilted slightly up and her eyes closed. Was she praying? Then John saw her smile . . . (pages 97 and 98).

Discussion: Talk about these sentences. What was Amy Carmichael feeling? How does the author show you?

Here's another example of *showing:*

> Something exploded inside John. In three running strides he tackled Jim and slammed him up against the wall. "You snake!" he cried, and slugged Jim in the jaw as hard as he could with his fist (page 84).

What was John feeling? What was he thinking? How does the author *show* this?

If each of these short segments only *told* what Amy Carmichael and John were thinking and feeling, what would they say? Prepare to be bored!

Now try a writing exercise using *show, don't tell.* On page 97, the court clerk announced the verdict in Jewel's case:

> "The court hereby orders Amy Carmichael, of Dohnavur Fellowship, to surrender the child in question to her legal guardian by April 4. . . ."

Write a paragraph showing John's reaction as he hears this terrible news. *Show* your readers what he thinks, feels, and experiences. Remember, actions, words, and description are tools for showing. (WRITING)

LIT/LA 13: We read this story from John's point of view. The authors use an important writing tool called "point of view" to tell the story through the main character's eyes. We see what John sees. We feel John's feelings and "hear" his thoughts. We experience Jewel's rescue as John experienced it.

Reread pages 99 through 106 in chapter 10. On these pages, readers travel with John to Dohnavur. We see John meeting Miss Beath. We experience John's thoughts and feelings as he hides in the dark, waiting. Finally, we feel amazed and afraid right along with John when Jewel comes out dressed as a boy.

What if a reader experienced these events from a different point of view? Turn this chapter on its head by rewriting this part of the story from Jewel's point of view. Tell how Jewel prepared to meet John in the dark outside Dohnavur. While John was renting an oxcart and hiding in the bushes, what was Jewel doing? While John was worrying about every sound and person, afraid of being discovered, what was Jewel feeling? Finally, *show* readers Jewel's experience as she and John drove away from Dohnavur in the oxcart. (WRITING)

LIT/LA 14: On page 113, John and his mother discuss the possible options for saving Jewel. Imagine you are part of that conversation. John says, *"England! We have to take her with us to England."* Or imagine his mother declaring, *"You return to England, and I'll find a place for her somewhere."* Or imagine John asking if Christians in Colombo could take her in and hide her.

Imagine the conversation between John and his mother as they try to solve this problem.

Remember, good writers *show* instead of merely telling. Good writers tell the story from the point of view of their main character. Good writers use action, dialogue, and description to show their main character's feelings, thoughts, and experiences.

So pick up your *show, don't tell* tools and write the story of John and his mother as they try to untangle this problem: What to do with Jewel? (WRITING)

The Church Today

 CT 1: Find www.trailblazerbooks.com on the Internet. This is the TRAILBLAZER BOOKS Web site. Click on the cover of *The Hidden Jewel* and you'll find maps, information about Amy Carmichael and Dohnavur, and a Web link giving information about the church in India today. (INTERNET)

 CT 2: Missionaries are not allowed in India today. Some Indian people want to pass laws forbidding Indian citizens to change their religion. In 1999 a Christian missionary, Aruldoss, was murdered. In many cities, billboards and posters openly ridicule Christianity. One poster shows a priest as a cat waiting to devour a congregation of mice. "Ban conversion," the poster reads.

Find out more about persecution of Christians in India and other countries online at www.persecutedchurch.org. Follow online links to other Web sites on this topic.

Take notes on what you learn to share in a discussion group in your class, family, or homeschool group. (INTERNET)

 CT 3: Go online at www.hungersite.org to learn about world hunger. In India and other poor countries, hunger is an everyday, every-hour problem. Children die of malnutrition. Families work but cannot even provide food for their children. (INTERNET)

 CT 4: Log on to www.j2000usa.org. See History Activities 6, 7, and 8 in this guide to learn about Jubilee 2000, an effort by Christians to help poor countries like India get out of debt. (INTERNET)

 CT 5: Contact World Vision at (800) 423-4200 and sponsor an Indian child. Child sponsorship is a simple, meaningful, effective way to help. (HANDS-ON)

MEGA PROJECT IDEAS: 6 and 7

 CT 6: Make a difference in India! Support a pastor-in-training. Buy a bicycle for a traveling evangelist. Send Bibles to churches and Christian schools.

How? Plan a group fund-raiser. Ask neighbors and community businesses to sponsor your group as you clean up a neighborhood park. Prepare and sell tickets to an Indian meal at your church or homeschool group. Hold a Saturday Work-for-India workday. Offer to do chores such as raking leaves, shoveling snow, cleaning garages, etc. for friends and church members in exchange for a donation to your "Make a Difference in India" project.

Where? Through Samaritan's Purse, a Christian program designed to give practical, needed help to Christians around the world. Just $20 will send an Indian man or woman to Bible School for a month. Or $90 will purchase a bicycle for an evangelist.

Contact Samaritan's Purse at (800) 663-6500 for information. (HANDS-ON)

 CT 7: Learn about the church in Amy Carmichael's land today. Read *The Secret Search,* a short exploration learning project about a real twenty-first century Muslim boy who searched for God. The project includes some learn-and-apply cultural and information-based activities designed to show Western Christians the challenge experienced by Islamic people who turn to Jesus. Call Crossroads at (408) 378-6658. (VIDEO)

Resources

Titles in bold indicate resources particularly recommended for supplementing this Curriculum Guide.

Online: The following Internet Web sites are mentioned in this guide:
  www.geocities.com/Athens/5180
  www.gospelmi.org
  www.hungersite.com
  www.intouch.org/INTOUCH/portraits/
    amy_carmichael.html
  www.j2000usa.org
  www.persecutedchurch.org.
  www.tamil.org
  www.trailblazerbooks.com

Organizations:
  World Vision: (800) 423-4200
  Samaritan's Purse: (800) 663-6500

Print: The following resources are mentioned in this guide:
  A Chance to Die: The Life and Legacy of Amy Carmichael by Elisabeth Elliot. Old Tappan, NJ: Fleming H. Revell Company, 1987.
  Amy Carmichael of Dohnavur by Frank L. Houghton. Fort Washington, PA: Christian Literature Crusade, 1979, 1985.
  Amy Carmichael: Rescuer of Precious Gems by Janet and Geoff Benge. Seattle, WA: YWAM, 1999.[1]
  Anni's India Diary by Anni Axworthy. Halesite, NY: Whispering Coyote Press, 1992.
  Bright Ideas! Wycliffe Bible Translators (missions related materials).[2]
  Enchantment of the World: India by Sylvia McNair. Danbury, CT: Children's Press, 1990.
  The First Rains by Peter Bonnici. Minneapolis: Carolrhoda Publishers, 1985.
  The Ganges by Michael Pollard. New York: Benchmark Books, 1998.

Gold Cord: The Story of a Fellowship by Amy Carmichael. London: Society for Promoting Christian Knowledge, 1932.
India by Michael Dahl. Mankato, MN: Bridgestone Books, 1998.
India: A Study of an Economically Developing Country by David Cumming. New York: Thomson, 1995.
India: The Culture by Bobbie Kalman. New York: Crabtree Publishing, 1990.
India: The Land by Bobbie Kalman. New York: Crabtree Publishing, 1990.
The Jungle Book by Rudyard Kipling. New York: Signet-Doubleday, 1981.
Just So Stories by Rudyard Kipling. New York: Puffin Books, 1994.
Mister and Me by Kimberly Willis Holt. New York: Putnam, 1998.
National Geographic. Washington, D.C.: National Geographic Society.[3]
Not Separate, Not Equal by Brenda Wilkinson. New York: Harper and Row, 1987.
Prank by Kathryn Lasky. New York: Dell, 1986.
Sarah With an H by Hadley Irwin. New York: McElderry, 1996.
Seasons of Splendor: Indian Folklore by Madhur Jaffrey. New York: Puffin Books, 1987.
The Secret Search. Campbell, CA: Crossroads Publications, 1998.[4]
The Sneetches by Dr. Suess. New York: Random House, 1961.
Something Beautiful for God by Malcolm Muggeridge. New York: Harper and Row, 1986.
Tales From the Jungle Book by Robin McKinley. New York: Random House, 1985.
Teenage Refugees and Immigrants From India Speak Out by R. Viswanath. New York: Rosen, 1997.

The Tiger's Whisker by Harold Courlander. New York: Henry Holt, 1995.

The Token Gift by Hugh McKibbon. New York: Firefly Books (U.S. Distributor), 1996.

Video: The following resources are mentioned in this guide:

Carol's Mirror, Mennonite Central Committee.[5]

Children Creating Peace, Mennonite Central Committee.[5]

The Great Indian Railway, National Geographic Videos, 1995.

Gandhi, TriStar Productions, 1997. Rated PG.

Something Beautiful for God, A PBS Video, 1973. (Try your local library or a rental store that carries classic videos.)

---

[1] Youth With a Mission Publishers may be reached at (800) 922-2143.

[2] Order these materials from Wycliffe Bible Translators at (800) WYCLIFFE.

[3] Articles and issues of *National Geographic* magazine listed in activity descriptions. Back issues: (800) 647-5463. Education Dept: (800) 368-2728 for additional resources.

[4] Available at (408) 378-6658.

[5] Available from Mennonite Central Committee at (715) 859-1151 (U.S.) or (888) 622-6337 (Canada).